SHAMELESS FLIRT

A HOPELESSLY BROMANTIC PRELUDE

LAUREN BLAKELY

own copy. Thank you for respecting the author's work.

ALSO BY LAUREN BLAKELY

Big Rock Series

Big Rock

Mister O

Well Hung

Full Package

Joy Ride

Hard Wood

Hopelessly Bromantic Duet (MM)

Hopelessly Bromantic

Here Comes My Man

Happy Endings Series

My Single-Versary

A Wild Card Kiss

Shut Up and Kiss Me

Kismet

Rules of Love Series

The Rules of Friends with Benefits (A Prequel

Always Satisfied Series

Satisfaction Guaranteed

Instant Gratification

Overnight Service

Never Have I Ever

PS It's Always Been You

Special Delivery

The Sexy Suit Series

Lucky Suit

Birthday Suit

From Paris With Love

Wanderlust

Part-Time Lover

One Love Series

The Sexy One

The Only One

The Hot One

The Knocked Up Plan

Come As You Are

Sports Romance

ABOUT

When my boss hits me with the news that I'll be working in London for a year, I say yes so fast. What could be better than a year abroad on the company's dime surrounded by swoony British men?

Meeting the sexiest, most charming man ever my first day in London — that's what.

But then I lose track of him in a crowd. No last name. No number.

Suddenly, finding him again feels like the most important thing I must do in my year abroad...

Shameless Flirt is a prequel in the Hopelessly Bromantic Duet and it leads into the full-length novel Hopelessly Bromantic. You don't have to read Shameless Flirt to enjoy Hopelessly Bromantic , but you'll likely enjoy this story before the story!

SHAMELESS FLIRT

BY LAUREN BLAKELY

A Hopelessly Bromantic Prelude

Don't want to miss a single delicious MM romance? Be sure to sign up for my MM mailing list!

1

BRING ON THE ZEPPELIN

Seven Years Ago

TJ

When my boss calls me into her office on Thursday afternoon, I anticipate nothing but the usual sort of assignment—cover a major staff shakeup at a TV network, or an imbroglio at some media giant. Copy due by five, of course.

I expect to be headed as far as

Midtown, not across the Atlantic Ocean.

"How would you like to work in London for the next year?" asks the no-nonsense newswoman, offering an opportunity I've dreamed of since I was thirteen.

A chance to go back to England?

Yes, please. More than anything.

Before I can close my gaping mouth to say as much, Ms. Deadline, as we call her, makes my answer irrelevant. She shakes her head with a curt laugh. "Actually, it's not really a question. We are sending you to London, TJ."

There's only one thing to say. "Can I leave today?"

I imagine exactly how it will go, picturing it like a movie montage.

The flight will entail the requisite number of unruly kids, all somehow seated in the row directly behind me. I will, of course, have to cram myself into a middle seat, which is no fun at six-three. While the future juvenile delin-quents kick the back of my chair for eight hours, the friendly lady next to me will chatter on about the Jell-O molds she's making for her Aunt Patty's eighty-fifth birthday party.

There will, of course, be turbulence.

Cut to me staring forlornly at the barren Heathrow baggage carousel. As my fellow passengers grab their suitcases and get on with their vacations or their reunions, the airline informs me they've lost my luggage. I'll spend my first night in the city with only the clothes I arrived in.

I'll roll with it. Shit happens, bags get lost, and it's my turn on the conveyor belt of bad fortune.

No biggie. At least I'll be unencumbered as I head to the flat I rented, where the leasing agent meets me to say there's been a wee bit of a mix-up concerning my living arrangements. Of course there has.

Instead of a sweet pad overlooking the river, my new residence is a dinky unfurnished studio, and one floor up is some crotchety old guy who plays bootleg Led Zeppelin records at all hours. The pipes will be creaky, the hot water finicky, and there won't be a decent coffee shop for miles.

And I won't care, no matter how much I dislike Led Zeppelin.

Because every dude in London will have an English accent.

Yes, please!

I pull myself back to the present and focus on my boss. "I can be on the next flight." I'm super helpful that way, particularly with opportunities that involve a potential panoply of swoony Brits.

"Love that attitude," Ms. Deadline says. "But let me give you the job details."

It seems that, after covering the business of TV, media, and advertising for 24News in New York, I'll now be reporting on the London financial markets. It's a positive step in my journalism career, and the company will provide relocation services and a furnished flat. I don't have to do a thing but pack my clothes.

Nice.

"This is a huge opportunity for someone so young, and we're offering it to you because we're truly impressed with your work." She stands and reaches across her impeccably neat desk, free of the usual journalist's mess, and shakes my hand. "You'll start in two weeks."

"Fantastic," I say, hoping the next fourteen days fly by. "I'll be ready."

Packing up my life is easy. I'm a nomad—give me a laptop and a phone, and I'm good to go. Well, I can't do without a couple of nice shirts and access to a gym. But other than that, I'm a guy with simple needs.

Everything complicated is in my head—like all my hopes and dreams— dreams I want to chase in London.

Well, when I'm not busy chasing men.

But I plan to make time for both.

2

HERE I COME

TJ

On Friday two weeks later, I'm more than ready to hit the road. Even my bags look eager to jet, parked by the door.

"And I'm outta here," I announce to my three roommates. For the last year, Trey, Nolan, Ashlee, and I have shared an extremely mediocre apartment in Queens, one that only the under twenty-five-and-dying-to-live-in-a-cool-city set consider inhabitable. Since that describes me and all my friends, there's a long list of guys and dolls ready to jump on a spare room. A friend of Ashlee's leaped first, and she'll be taking my room tonight.

As I hoist my carry-on bag onto my shoulder, Ashlee keeps shooting zombies on the Xbox. Trey is knitting an argyle sweater vest for a cat. Nolan whips up a mushroom omelet at the stove.

"Try not to miss me while I'm gone," I call out.

"Don't worry. We won't," Ashlee says as she takes out a nest of the undead. "Not until we need someone to fix the sink."

"You'll be crying for your resident handyman then," I reply.

"You'll send us a how-to video, though," Ashlee shouts over the splatter.

"I will . . . *if* you send me a pizza from John's of Bleecker Street. I'll pine for their cheese pies more than anything while I'm gone." I turn toward the kitchen. "Well, maybe not more than Nolan's cooking."

My bespectacled friend and I share a nod of mutual appreciation. "And I'll miss your sarcasm, TJ."

"It's a good thing we're both great at something," I say, heading his way.

Nolan turns off the burner and steps away from the stove, and I give my college bud a quick clap on the back. "Have fun, and good luck with your mission," he says.

I stare at him in confusion. "What mission?"

"Dude, I've known you since freshman year. I know what you want to do in London, and I bought you a goodbye gift." Nolan reaches for a Duane Reade bag on the kitchen counter and tosses it to me.

I peer inside and laugh. "Aww. I'll miss you most of all, Scarecrow," I say and hug the box of condoms to my chest.

Then, it's time to go.

I leave the keys on the entryway

table for the next roommate, and I take off for my new adventure.

My identical twin waits for me on the street. Since Chance is catching a flight to Florida, we're sharing a ride to the airport. Plus, it's extra time to say goodbye.

When my brother sees my luggage, he laughs. I've got only one carry-on and only one suitcase to check, and my younger-by-five-minutes brother is obviously *not* shocked. Once we're in the taxi, he whips out his phone, clicks open his notes app, and thrusts it out so I can read it. "Called it," he says.

The note—with a timestamp to prove it—is a spot-on prediction. *For one year abroad: one carry-on, one check in.*

I laugh. "You know me so well. It's almost like we share DNA." Chance has only his overnight bag on the seat next to him as the yellow car peels out of Queens.

"I also predict you'll come home with a million books," Chance says. "I remember when we were thirteen and Mom and Dad took us to London. You lugged home that entire suitcase full of paperbacks. We stopped in at that bookshop on Cecil Court, and you came out with so many books we had to drop them at the hotel before heading to Westminster Abbey."

I've given most of those books away by now—the story of international teen spy Rhys Locke and the Hollywood bonkbusters from Caroline Vienna—but when I was an awkward, gangly teen, I devoured them and plotted a future. "I remember that bookshop fondly, and I plan to go back," I say. "Maybe it'll be my first stop."

On the ride to JFK, we chat about our goals for the next few months, something we've always done since we were kids—sharing hopes and dreams. Now a ballplayer in his second year in the majors, Chance will be on the road a lot, pitching for the San Francisco Cougars, and he wants to establish himself as their closer, he says.

As for me, I want . . . a lot of things.

Things I haven't admitted out loud to anyone.

I glance out the cab window, watching New York whip by. Will I miss this city when I'm overseas? I've always longed to experience different places, meet different people. More than that, I've wanted to create places and people for others to experience. I want to create something out of all the experiences I take in.

That last one, though, feels so personal and lives so close to my heart that I haven't even dared to tell my brother, who knows me better than anyone. I didn't share the idea when I was thirteen as it first took root. Not sure if I'm ready to voice it now.

"What about you?" Chance prompts in a lull in the conversation. He's told me about his vision for himself as a pitcher. I suppose that means it's my turn to crack open my heart.

Easier said than done.

I scratch my jaw and shrug. "Oh, you

know. Try to grow a beard, eat some fish and chips, meet a hot dude. The usual."

Chance rolls his eyes. "Liar."

"What?" I protest. "That's all true."

"Yes, I know. But so are the things you're *not* saying," he says with certainty.

"Twin intuition?"

"Something like that."

"What am I not saying, then?" I counter stubbornly.

He shoots me a *no-bullshit* stare. "There's something else you want, TJ."

I blow out a breath, wishing he didn't read me so well. Sometimes it's just simpler to keep your dreams to yourself. Chance's goals are different. It's a lofty ambition, being the closing pitcher for a professional baseball team, but he's already on a team as a relief pitcher. Maybe it's a tall ladder, but he's on a rung.

My dreams seem so out of reach. Like, oceans and mountains away. Maybe galaxies.

But I don't like being dishonest with Chance, so I carve out a portion of the truth. "I'd like to be the best damn reporter I can be. I want to impress the hell out of 24News. Get bigger and better assignments. Tell stories readers can't put down."

There. That's true enough.

Chance nods, seeming pleased with that answer. "I have faith in you."

"Thanks." I hope his faith is enough for both of us.

Clearing his throat, he reaches into the side pocket of his overnight bag. "I got you something," he says a touch awkwardly. I know it's not his style to give going-away gifts.

"Aww, I take back all the times I said you weren't a nice guy," I tease. Snarky is easier than serious.

Without acknowledging my comment, he fishes out a book. Wait. No. It's more like . . . a journal. He doesn't hand it to me, though. He holds it close to his chest like it's precious, just like he cradles the ball when he's on the pitcher's mound.

I press pause on the sarcasm button, looking from the journal to my brother as he speaks.

"When we were in London with Mom and Dad, you kept a journal," he says. "You read it out loud to me every night. By which I mean you read it in that TV announcer voice you use when you're pretending something isn't important."

I nod a little solemnly. "I remember. I called it *Bedtime Reading*."

You wrote funny stories about what we did each day but added your own twist. How when we visited Buckingham Palace, the queen was probably sneaking away to eat Cap'n Crunch in a stateroom to plot heists while the prince was busy doing something secretive."

The memory amuses me, especially since I know what the prince was off doing. I just didn't read that part to him at that age. "I had an active imagination."

"Bet you still do."

Chance is quiet for a spell, and so am I. Maybe we're both lost in time.

Then he goes on. "When we were back home," he says, "you'd be in your room at night reading mystery and romance novels. But sometimes, you still wrote in that travel journal."

Whoa. Someone notices everything. "You do have twin-tuition," I say, and that's as much of an admission as I can manage.

With a nod, he hands me the light blue notebook. There's an illustration of Tower Bridge on it and a passport stamp in the corner. "Maybe you'll keep a travel journal while you're there this time. Maybe it'll inspire you."

It's weighty when I take it, like this is *the* gift he's wanted to give me for years. I flip open the cover, the blank pages a gorgeous invitation to fill them.

I turn the journal over to find a price tag, worn thin over the years. The number is faded, the store name smudged, only the *O* and *B* still visible.

Is it from the same shop? The one with a brick exterior, bright white walls, and a clock that looks like the moon?

I meet my brother's gaze. "You got this when we were kids?"

With a smile, he answers, "At that same store. I held on to it till the right moment."

Wow. I'm all but speechless. "Thanks, Chance." It's sincere, not a bit of snark. I hug him to let him know how touched I am. "I'll definitely start writing in this today."

At JFK, we grab our bags and head into the terminal, stopping under a big departure sign. This is where he goes to Florida to pitch against the Miami team, and I go to London for the new phase of my career.

We glance at the screen then turn to each other. Chance flashes a wide grin. "Have fun, but don't let anyone break your heart while you're in London living out your fantasy."

"Please. There will be no heartache. Only good times. And you—" I pat his chest. "You'll be the closer in no time."

He gazes heavenward with crossed fingers. I laugh and cuff his shoulder. "Maybe I'll miss you a tiny bit."

"I recorded you saying that," he whispers. "Now I have leverage over you forever."

I narrow my eyes with a warning. "Don't fuck with someone who looks just like you."

"Good point," Chance admits, then we take a selfie and say goodbye and head our separate ways.

Shoulders back, head up, I make for the international concourse. This is the life. Young, single, and with only me to worry about.

For now, I put aside the bigger dreams, the ones I'll write about in this journal. I'll deal with them once I settle into a new city in about twelve hours.

First things first. Here I come, shitty

flight, Led Zeppelin-blasting neighbors, and horrid brown water.

Bring it on. Because everything at the top of my "to-do in London" list will come after-hours.

And so will I.

TESTING WITH STRANGERS

TJ

My fortune-telling was only slightly off in that the airline didn't *lose* my bag. They know exactly where it is. That place just doesn't happen to be *here*.

"It seems your bag, Mister Ashford, popped off the JFK flight and hopped onto the cart for the Istanbul one," the customer service agent chirps, describing my suitcase's gymnastics as if it were a naughty little tyke, stealing away from its family.

I'm exhausted from the flight and

raring to get the hell out of here. But I'm also keenly aware of caricatures. The last thing I want is to come across like a giant American jackass, so I decide to lean into her cheery style.

You catch more flies with honey and all.

"Yes"—I glance at her name tag— "Louise. It does seem to have a mind of its own."

"And perhaps a longing to see Turkey?" she suggests helpfully.

"Understandable," I say, then glance behind me. The lost luggage office is empty so I keep up the convo, hoping it helps my cause. "I've always wanted to visit Istanbul. Can't blame my luggage if it wants to take a spin through the Blue Mosque and the Grand Bazaar."

She smiles sympathetically. "I do apologize, and we'll have it on its way here soon. We can send it to your hotel or your place of residence."

"That'd be great." I flash a friendly smile. "Any idea when?"

"Excellent question." She peers at the

monitor in front of her. "Your globe-trotting bag is . . . wait. Hold on. Apparently, it's on its way to Brussels first, and *then* to Turkey. We can send it back on a direct flight from Istanbul to Heathrow tomorrow."

"My stowaway is taking the scenic route," I say.

"Imagine the stories it can tell when it returns." She then slides me a piece of paper. "Here's a voucher for a free drink on your next flight."

"Thanks. I appreciate this," I say, but I appreciate something else too—her storytelling. She might be the perfect audience, so I decide to float a test balloon. I clear my throat. "If I ever write a novel with a gate agent who goes above and beyond to make a traveler laugh, I'll call her Louise."

Whew. That felt a little weird, like speaking a new language. But it felt good too, sharing the start of something that matters to me.

She pats her name tag. "I would be honored."

I take the drink coupon and add it to my carry-on, then head outside, where I pause to breathe in the English air.

I hail a taxi, and when the black car pulls up and I climb inside, the driver asks, "Where to, sir?"

I give him the address of the hotel where I'll be staying before moving into my flat tomorrow. As the cab pulls away from the curb, I surreptitiously sniff my shirt. I could use a shower. A second later, a jaw-cracking yawn says a shower isn't the only thing I need. Jet lag wallops me, and my eyes float closed.

The next thing I hear is the squeal of tires as the driver brakes then acceler-ates, darting through London traffic.

I rub my eyes, turning my head from side to side to stare out the windows. A red double-decker bus obscures the view to the right, but on the left, a steady stream of people files out of the Piccadilly Circus Underground Station and onto the street. I must have snoozed the whole way into the city.

A grin takes me hostage at the sights around me. This is not a tourist grin. This is not a bright-eyed and bushy-tailed smile. This is the optimism of opportunity.

A deep *rightness* settles over me, the sense I'm where I'm meant to be.

Ever since my visit ten years ago, I've wanted to return, to experience London in new ways. I want to learn its secrets, maybe even unravel some of my own. I want to sit on a park bench and stare at the gardens as words and worlds unfold in my head. Or maybe I'll grab a seat in a coffee shop and look out the window at the rain and then the fog while I'm off somewhere else in my mind, spinning a tale.

"Looks like we're right in the heart of London," I say to the cabbie as the traffic slows to a crawl.

"Indeed. Almost there." The driver turns toward the hotel, the sign above the roundabout entrance beckoning. "What brings you to London?"

That's a simple enough question.

"Work. I write for a news organization, and I'm relocating to the branch here."

"Excellent. Make sure to check out Big Ben if you're not working too hard," he says. "And the London Eye."

"Definitely," I say as he pulls up in front of the hotel entrance.

It's one-thirty on a Saturday. My fingers grip the handle of the cab door, ready to open it so I can climb out, but an impulse seizes me. It's an urge to take a step further than I did with Louise, to say what I didn't tell my brother on the way to the airport in New York.

The words should have come easily with Chance, but they didn't. The thought of voicing this goal to family and friends, to colleagues and even acquaintances—is terrifying. I don't want to disappoint anyone, especially since I'm pretty sure I'll disappoint myself.

But a stranger won't pin hopes on me. I can't let down a stranger.

I turn back to the driver and say, "And I want to write a novel."

The man smiles. "No better place," he says.

I breathe easier when I get out of the cab with my carry-on. I feel lighter. There, I said it.

Now, I have to do it.

4

BONER AT FIRST SIGHT

TJ

First, I'll brush my teeth.

That's my plan as I enter the hotel. Next, I'll stand under a hot shower for a decadently long time and wash the flight off me.

Only, I won't be doing either of those things in the immediate future.

"Your room isn't ready yet, sir." The front desk attendant informs me when I try to check in.

I groan. Maybe I could just flop into

an exhausted heap on the floor. But um, hello, terrible caricature of a traveler.

Instead, I paste on a smile. "When do you think it'll be available?"

The gray-haired man behind the desk checks his watch then smiles. "At three o'clock on the dot."

That's an hour and a half from now.

Don't mope.

Don't groan.

"Cool," I say. "Any place I can shower?"

"No, but you can freshen up in the loo."

He says it like such a solution might never have occurred to me. As it happens, I'm familiar with indoor plumbing and appreciative of its utility vis-à-vis *freshening up.*

I can wash my face and slay my dragon breath with a toothbrush, but I can't shower. At least, not until three o'clock on the dot. And even then, I don't have a change of clothes. I can't cruise the streets of London in the same jeans and T-shirt I've worn for too many hours and on two continents.

So, I turn to the clerk with this next order of business. "Also, the airline sent my luggage on a detour, so it's going to arrive here tomorrow. Do you know where I could shop for a new shirt and some boxer briefs?"

Trouble is, the guy is sixty, at least, and I think I saw a suit like that on a BBC show from the seventies. Small chance he'll know what a twenty-something queer dude would wear on a night out in London.

"Like, a cool shop. Where the millennials go," I add, hoping that makes it clear I mean "Not a grandpa store."

He thinks for a moment then says, helpfully, "There's a TK Maxx around the corner."

It's a place to start, I guess. Maybe I'll give it a shot then hit up Google if I have no luck.

After I brush my teeth and splash water on my face in the *men's room*—I refuse to call it a loo—I leave my carry-on with the bellhop and set out for the store.

When I walk through Manhattan, I usually listen to music. But I know all the corners and alleys of New York. I want to take in London with all my senses—see it *and* hear it. So, after a quick look at a map, I stuff my phone in my front pocket.

I head across the street, listening to the sounds of my new home—the rumble of buses, the honk of horns, the rustle of Londoners coming and going right along with me. I'm part of the city's current, the American in jeans and a No Name band T-shirt—literally, that's the band's name.

The route to the store takes me through Piccadilly Circus. As I pass the Shaftesbury Memorial Fountain, glancing at the statue of the winged dude with a bow and arrow, I decide that the hero in my novel should kiss someone by the fountain.

Cliché? Maybe. Or maybe not.

No one whose lover wanted to kiss him by a fountain ever rolled his eyes and said it was too cliché. Fountains are perfect for kisses. Some clichés are clichés because they're true.

I turn on the next street and spot the store at the end of the block. But when I'm close enough to scan the window displays, everything looks terribly familiar.

The name TK Maxx should have been a dead giveaway. I let out the biggest *ugh* of disdain. "That is literally just a British T.J. Maxx."

I say it to myself, but a man chuckles nearby. "Indeed, you're not wrong," he says.

Are you kidding me?

This can't be happening. There is no way a British magazine model has stopped to talk to me. No way is *this* the first guy my age I meet in old Blighty. He's all carved cheekbones, full lips, thick blond hair, and cool blue eyes that see inside my soul.

Okay, I'm exaggerating. My psyche

isn't cellophane, and he doesn't have X-ray vision, but . . . yum.

"It's our discount shop," the English guy says, pulling a messenger bag onto his shoulder. "It has a little bit of everything."

I'd like a little bit of him.

I search my exhausted brain for something borderline witty. "I might be in the market for a little bit of every-thing," I say, grateful for toothpaste and men's rooms and no dragon breath. "Where should I start at TK Maxx?"

The guy tilts his head to consider the storefront for a moment, then glances back at me. "Depends on what you're looking for. They have surpris-ingly fashionable dog clothes, excellent popcorn, and also home furnishings."

"Good to know in case I get a late-night craving." I linger on that last word. If he bats for my team, it won't hurt to flirt a bit. "For popcorn," I finish. Then I shift to practical matters and tug at my shirt. "But first, I'm on the hunt for a new shirt."

"Ah, clothes." He steps a little closer, gesturing to what I'm wearing. "You might try Angie's Vintage Duds around the corner, if that's your thing. They have cool retro tees and stuff."

Do they have you? Do you want to be my shopping assistant?

But I know better than to ask out a random guy on the street.

Especially since I doubt the gods of luck, or kissing fountains, or horny dudes, would deposit the world's most handsome man in front of me in London and say, *"Guess what, TJ? He also likes dick!"*

That's not how life works, regardless of the way he waved at my chest, regardless of the way he stepped closer.

I will not be making out with this guy in front of the winged statue. Not ever.

Because *that's* how fantasy works, and this is real life.

"Thanks," I say, steering for the reality lane. "I'll keep this place in mind if I need a new vest for my dog and maybe hit up Angie's for a shirt. You never know who you might meet on your first day in London."

I add a small smile.

A friendly smile. Not a come-on smile.

He lifts a brow. Those blue eyes twinkle. "That's true. You never know." For a fraction of a second, his teeth scrape the corner of his full lip, a move that stirs all my parts. "By the way," he says, "I'm Jude. I work at a bookshop on Cecil Court."

And then . . .?

He turns on his heel and walks away.

Did that just happen? Did the magazine model truly invite me to find him where he works? Which just happens to be my favorite childhood bookstore?

This is like fate. This is something I would totally write:

Gorgeous Brit invites grubby American to a bookstore—

I hit the brakes on the mental madness. I must have imagined that lip bite. Surely, I'm making more of this moment than I ought to.

I'll just enjoy the fading view and that will be that.

Bleary-eyed, I stare at the handsome figure blending into the sea of Londoners. Just as I turn toward Angie's, Jude turns too, and looks my way.

And this time, I let myself believe this is real.

5

SECRET HANDSHAKE

TJ

Eggplant Helen is the most helpful person I've met in my entire life.

She's the shop manager of Angie's Vintage Duds, who introduced herself as that when I walked in. *I'm Aubergine Helen. Eggplant Helen for an American,* she said as she flicked her purple hair.

Now, she's already hand-selected three shirts for me and set them on the hook in the dressing room.

"Go in. Try them on." She gently pushes me through the heavy red curtain. "I'll tell you which looks best for your first night in town."

Inside, I tug off my shirt. "How did you know I was going out tonight?"

"Young American lad like you, course you're going out. Besides, Angie's has the coolest clothes, and I don't think you came here to shop so you could stay in all by your lonesome." Then she claps twice, a *move along* sort of sound. "All right. Show me what you've got."

I step out of the dressing room and model a shirt she picked. It has an illustration of a Tetris game on it. Retro, indeed.

"Perfect. It looks good. That is, if you like that kind of fit, nice and snug?" Her voice pitches up, waiting for my input.

If she's my stylist for my first night out, she should know what I dig. "Well, I like it . . . if the guys I meet like it too."

"Good to know." Her arm darts into the dressing room and comes out with the other shirts. "These won't do, then.

Not snuggly enough." She scurries around the shop like The Energizer Bunny, returning with a couple more options. "These will better fit your style."

"I have a style?" My wardrobe is pretty uneventful. Jeans, blue button-downs for work, the occasional polo, and a few band tees.

Helen shudders. "No. But we'll soon change that. I'll have you turned out positively fetching, and *you'll* have all the lads eating out of the palm of your hand."

"I came to the right place," I say, pretty damn pleased.

She tips her head to the door, a knowing look in her eyes. "We're LGBTQ-friendly. Angie is married to a woman."

"Cool. That's awesome. All of that," I say. But especially awesome is the part I keep in my head.

This might be the writer in me, finding motives in coincidence, but could Jude have sent me *here* because he caught on that I like dudes? Could it mean he does too?

Yeah, TJ, that's it. The hot Brit sent you on a scavenger hunt to a gay-friendly shop as a secret handshake inviting you into Pink London.

Sighing, I shake my head at myself. I need some sleep, or I'll be imagining cryptic passwords and rainbow illuminati.

I yank the dressing room curtain closed and change into a tee with *The Dude Abides* stretching over my pecs. *The Big Lebowski* makes this a no-brainer yes.

As I pull on the next shirt, my brain turns to mulling over the scavenger hunt notion again. On one hand, it's ridiculous to think Jude sent me here on purpose and equally ridiculous to think he invited me to his store.

Yet, on the other hand, I keep coming back to the idea. Does that mean there's something to it?

Something besides wishful thinking?

I shake off the thought and put on my old black tee, then grab the shirts and meet Helen by the racks. "I'll take all three."

"Wonderful," Eggplant Helen says as she ushers me to the register. "Now, I know I'm not your target market, but you did look quite scrummy in the Tetris one, so I bet you'll attract the locals in that, no problem."

If I've learned anything today, it's the ease of talking to strangers—no one judges you, or if they do, it doesn't matter.

"Helen, can I ask your advice?" I venture.

"I sure wish you would."

I check that there are no customers in earshot; I don't want to sound like an idiot. "I heard about your store when I was standing outside TK Maxx."

She grimaces. "That place is ghastly for clothes."

"You're not wrong. But while I was there, this guy . . ." I pause, and her eyes say *tell me more*. "This very handsome guy stopped and mentioned your shop and suggested I shop here."

Her eyebrows shoot toward her hairline. "And then?" She beckons with her fingers for me to give her more. "I want every detail."

"And then he happened to mention his name."

She gasps.

"And that he worked at a bookstore on Cecil Court," I add.

Helen vibrates with enthusiasm like a chihuahua at dinnertime. "Take these shirts. Slap on some cologne. Go change and get moving to that bookstore."

I laugh, trying to stifle my hope, but I'm not sure I'm successful at hiding how excited I am. "You think so?"

She stares at me sternly. "Why else would he mention where he worked? Drop the tidbit of his name? Send you here? Off you go!" She stuffs the shirts into a plastic bag, thrusts it at me, and points to the door. "But report back tomorrow. I do fancy myself a matchmaker," she adds in a confessional whisper.

"I can tell, and I will report back. I promise." I take a step toward the door then turn back when I remember, "I also need a strong coffee. But nothing from an American chain, please. Their coffee is like drinking burnt sadness."

"And ours is like drinking watered-down malaise. Best to learn that harsh lesson sooner rather than later. But an English Breakfast tea is like a shot in the arm. Ought to wake you right up."

Once I leave, I swing back to TK Maxx. I do need boxer briefs, and consignment isn't my preference for those. Then, I pop into a café and order an English Breakfast tea.

With that jolt of caffeine, I return to my hotel where my room is ready, and so is the shower.

Maybe the gods of horny young men are looking out for me.

6

TRICK ADDRESS

TJ

I forgot an important detail about Cecil Court, and when I round the corner into the famous alley, I stop in my tracks and stare slack-jawed.

I'm that guy—the one duped by a transposed phone number or a fake name. The guy who goes to the address Mister Perfect gave him, and oops! It's an empty lot! It's a sewage plant! Or . . . surprise! There are twenty fucking bookshops on Cecil Court.

Time fooled me over the years,

erasing all the other shops on this street. Or maybe at thirteen, the only place that existed for me was the nameless one where I whiled away hours in a corner, lost in a story.

Desire pulled a fast one on me today. As Cecil Court unfolds before me in all its very London, very quaint beauty, I feel like an idiot for thinking I might find him.

That Jude should want me to.

And I won't be that fool.

This is not some movie where I knock on all the doors or drop into all the bookshops, look for the chiseled blond with the cover model looks and the butter-melting voice.

This isn't a story where he pops out, waves, and invites me over for a pint.

No, this is real life. I'm the guy who lost his luggage and stupidly thought he scored a date. Who showered and put on a Tetris shirt and went on a quest with a pointless clue.

Silly me. Jet lag made me forget that real dates have times and places. Jude didn't give me a time or a place. He didn't ask me out.

I'm just a guy chasing after a shame-less flirt.

But I'm here now, and I'd always planned to stop by Cecil Court. I wander down the street, figuring I'll find the shop I went to as a kid.

That is all I'm looking for. I won't stare into every window display, peer around the shelves. Won't go to a counter and ask, *Does Jude work here?*

No fucking way.

On this cozy street, I feel like I've slipped back in time to Victorian England, with streetlamps and old-fashioned wooden signs hanging outside the shops. I stroll past the first few, but none sport the bright white shelves or the big clock that looks like the moon.

I make my way down the lane, swinging my gaze from left to right. It's not this one with antique maps in the window.

Not that one with the science textbooks.

And it's not this shop with bunnies and pirates on the book covers on display.

But maybe, just maybe, it's that store near the end of the lane.

Bright light emanates from within, and the brick exterior feels familiar. My pace quickens, my heart beating a little faster.

When I near the store, I spot the sign. *An Open Book*.

O and *B*, like on the smudged price tag on the travel journal.

With a burst of youthful glee, I push open the door and glance around the quiet shop teeming with books.

This is why I'm in London—to write articles for 24News and to start that novel. To become what I first imagined in this store.

I make my way farther in, and I'm checking out the Oscar Wildes when the thud of a heavy book hitting a shelf makes me turn.

My pulse spikes.

I blink.

Jude is here, putting a book away. He's stopped to stare straight at me, his lips twitching with the hint of a grin, his blue eyes full of mischief. "You found the shop," he says.

Everything feels a little heady, a lot possible.

It feels as though this is the start of something.

I don't answer right away. I let the words form in my head first, and then on my lips. "Well, I had a few clues."

Maybe I did step off the plane and into my very own rom-com.

TJ AND JUDE'S EPIC ROMANCE BEGINS IN Hopelessly Bromantic!
Order now while this epic romance is on a preorder discount!

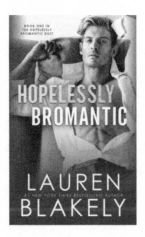

Want to be the first to hear about new MM releases? Sign up for my exclusive MM mailing list!

Read on for a preview of Hopelessly Bromantic!

TJ

Some Guys Are Just Like That
Present Day

Seven years ago, when my boss hit me with the news that he was sending me to London for the next twelve months, I could picture my nights unfolding like a dirty fairy tale.

After working my ass off all day, I'd hit the music bars, check out cool new bands, and meet hot guys. They'd charm me with their accents, and I'd charm them with my wit, and we'd bang till Big Ben struck morning O-O-O-and-one-more-O'clock.

My sex life would be nothing like it was in college, which was a lot like a drought—a famine from which, two years post-graduation, I'd only recently started to emerge.

But Ye Olde London? It would be a beefeater feast.

And sure, yeah, a great work opportunity. Obviously. And I wanted that because I had goals. Big ones.

Little ones too.

First, I wanted to stop at the bookstore on Cecil Court I went to on a family trip when I was an awkward teenager. While my parents hunted for a guidebook, I browsed the paperbacks, and for the first time in my life, I visualized my name on a cover. I left there with an armload of books . . . and a dream.

The bookshop was one of the first places I went when I arrived in London seven years ago. I wanted an auspicious beginning to my year abroad. Full circle and all that.

But that time, when I reached Cecil Court, it wasn't a paperback that sparked my dreams.

It was a man.

This bloke had more charm and appeal than any hero I could write into a novel.

But he wasn't simply between the covers of a story, where I could mastermind the ending. He was vibrant, real, and the most thrilling time I'd ever had. Soon, my London life was full of him.

And—spoiler alert—this guy in the bookstore was going to upend my world, not once, but twice.

Some guys were like that. They

stayed with you, even when you wanted them out of your head.

And they left, even when you wanted them to stay.

Chapter One
What Kind of Lap Dances Does He Like?

Jude

This is the greatest vacuum cleaner ever. There has never been a better one in all the land. It's literally going to change your life.

I repeat those notes from my agent before I head into the audition room—a drab, windowless shoebox of a place above a strip club on the outskirts of Leicester Square.

I've got no problem with the business of exotic dancing. But all things being equal, I'd rather audition for a new commercial above, say, a Tesco or an insurance office.

But a gig is a gig is a gig.

I put on my best smile as I give the casting director my name. "Jude Graham with Premier Talent. Harry Atkinson reps me, and it's a pleasure to be here."

The casting director looks up from her tablet, question marks in her eyes. "Harry? I thought he was—" She makes a slashing gesture against her throat.

"I hope not. I saw him a week ago. Very much alive. And also, not headless."

"Ah, must have been someone else," she says.

Yes, I've noticed the epidemic of talent-agent beheadings in London lately.

"Sorry for whoever that might be," I add.

She smiles faintly, the thick coat of plum lipstick cracking. "All right, show us you're in the market for a Cleaneroo."

Somehow, she manages to keep a straight face when she says the brand name—something I'll be required to do in *three, two, one . . .*

I become a cheerful, British businessman returning home to his flat after a hard day at the office. "Sweetheart, I swear the floors have never been prettier. Did you get that new Cleaneroo?"

Could this script be any more 1950s?

"Thank you," the casting director says, revealing zilch about how I did.

"Thank you for having me," I say with a gentlemanly nod as old-fashioned as this script.

Shit.

That was more of a bow. I meant to be jaunty, not obsequious. No matter. She didn't even notice. She's dragging her chipped red fingernail on the tablet screen, already done with me.

I grab my messenger bag and make my way down the rickety stairs in the back of the building, heading out through the strip club. A brunette dancer weaves past me, pink thigh-high boots jacking her up several inches, white seashells covering maybe half her breasts. An unlit cigarette dangles from her lips as she gives me a once-over. "Fancy a lap dance? Half off for you . . . I like blonds," she says.

"Thanks, but I'm on a lap-dance fast," I say, making my way to the exit.

Once I hit the street, I call my agent. "Why do these Cleaneroo people think you're dead, Harry?"

He chortles. "Ah, that's so typical of Vicki. When I don't send her anyone for a while, she assumes I've kicked the bucket."

That's not the most reassuring answer. But last year, Harry did book me a sweet spot that's still paying the bills, so I let rumors of his demise slide. "Maybe let her know you're still alive?"

"Oh, I already told her, Jude. She just called."

I perk up. That has to be good. "Did I get a callback already? I can turn around right now. Or is it even better? Did I get the job?" Antiquated gender stereotypes aside, I wouldn't mind the money.

"She said you look too much like Apollo. The Greek god."

What the hell does that mean? "Is that a good thing?"

"Of course it is," he says, too chipper to trust. "But they think you're too good-looking to peddle a vacuum. Like, no one believes you'd think about anything besides abs or kale smoothies, let alone cleaning. So it's a compliment, in a way . . ."

I sigh. "And, also, kind of not."

"It's a double-edged sword—your godly good looks."

I'm not sure what to say to that. "Should I forgo showers for a few days ahead of time for the next audition?"

He laughs. "Chin up. We'll find some more commercials for you soon. But in the meantime, the body spray people just sent a residual."

"Well, there's that double-edged

sword too." I played a complete douche in that advert, spraying Hammer Body Spray on my armpits before I sauntered into a nightclub. "Thanks, Harry."

I hang up and check the time. I'm not due at An Open Book for a half hour, but I might as well head over. Too bad the Cleaneroo commercial flopped —I rearranged my schedule at the store today to do that audition. *C'est la vie.*

I pop in my earbuds and tune into Carrie Fisher's memoir—someday, I'd like to have a secret affair with someone like Harrison Ford—as I make my way to Cecil Court. I turn down the next street, and there's no way I can miss the strapping man on the corner, staring up at the TK Maxx sign. He looks perturbed and, also, really fucking hot, with a strong jaw and thick dark hair.

A brooding sort of stuntman, he's all casual in jeans and a black T-shirt, no pretenses.

Time to take out my earbuds right now.

He sighs in frustration, flings a hand at the store.

"It's literally the British equivalent of T.J. Maxx," he mutters.

He's loud enough for me to hear and American enough for my happy radar to beep. I happen to be a connoisseur of American accents.

I stop a few feet from him. "It is, indeed," I agree. I've heard that about this shop, and I'm so bloody helpful to lumberjack-like men.

He turns, giving me a full, close-up view. *Those eyes*. Fuck me with a ten-inch dildo—they are a dreamy chocolate-brown with gold flecks.

I am not walking away.

I will continue this conversation for as long as I possibly can, or until I learn what kind of lap dances he likes. "It's our discount shop. It has a little bit of everything," I say.

He doesn't answer right away. Maybe he's straight. Sadder things have happened to me today.

"What do you know?" he asks in a

voice that sounds like he just got out of bed after having sex.

I like that image—a *lot*.

His dark eyes flicker, perhaps with dirty deeds. Maybe he's got the same images running through his head that I do. "I might be in the market for a little bit of everything," he adds. "Where should I start at TK Maxx?"

How about letting me show you around?

But best to make certain he's into the same things I am before getting too flirty. "Depends on what you're looking for. They have surprisingly fashionable dog clothes, excellent popcorn, and also home furnishings," I say, starting with a bit of charm.

His lips tilt into a bit of a grin as if I've entertained him. "Good to know, in case I get a late-night craving."

I've got a craving right now, all right.

The American gestures to his shirt. "But I'm on the hunt for a new shirt."

I wave a hand at his firm chest. "You might want to try Angie's Vintage Duds around the corner if that's your thing.

They have cool retro tees and stuff," I say while I cycle through tactics to get his number.

To satisfy my craving.

"Thanks. Maybe I'll hit up Angie's. You never know who you might meet your first day in London."

He shoots me a smile.

Trouble is, it's only a friendly one, not quite a come-and-get-me one.

I'm getting ahead of myself. I should get on my way because I don't usually hit on men on the street. Maybe the thing to do is leave him a clue and put the ball in his court.

"True. You never know." I pause for a moment, then . . . What the hell. You're only young once. "By the way, I'm Jude. I work at a bookshop on Cecil Court."

With that, I turn and get on my way, and I don't look back.

Not until I reach the end of the street. Then, I can't resist one more glance his way.

He hasn't moved, except to turn his

face toward me, watching me walk away.

A kernel of warmth spreads in my chest, and I know later, at the shop, I'll be staring at the door, hoping he walks in.

A few minutes later, as I reach Cecil Court, I realize what a daft idiot I am.

I didn't tell him *which* store I work in, and there are *only* twenty bookshops on this street. I check my watch. I can make it to Angie's to correct my mistake and still be on time for my shift. Spinning around, I walk quickly to Angie's. But as I peer in the window for a few long seconds, I only see the purple-haired woman who works there. I give her a wave, then head off.

Sigh. Another tiny heartbreak today, since I've a better chance of selling a Cleaneroo than seeing the American again.

Chapter Two

TJ's Travel Journal
London, Day One

My life was not a rom-com today.

It's been more like a manifestation of Murphy's Law. Everything that could go wrong on my trip to London did go wrong. The flight was cramped, turbulence hit an 8.0 on the Richter scale, then the airline lost my luggage. On top of that, the hotel said it wouldn't have my room ready for another few hours. I was tempted to crumple into a jet-lagged ball of stinky misery on the rundown lobby floor. I smelled like a ripe, day-old T-shirt, and I felt like a zombie. The front desk attendant took pity on me and sent me to a nearby store to buy some new clothes.

THANKS, FATE, FOR CHOOSING THAT EXACT MOMENT TO SEND ME THE WORLD'S MOST BEAUTIFUL MAN.

When Jude gave me his name then

walked away, my life was distilled into two choices:

Go to every single bookstore on Cecil Court and find him.

Or miss out on what felt like the first chapter in my new life here in England.

Wait. There was a third choice. Get my ass over to the thrift store he recommended, buy some new clothes, and then beg, borrow or steal for a shower if I had to.

I was not going to let this chance pass me by.

Cecil Court, here I come.

Chapter Three
We Meet Again

TJ

When I wander down the little lane in Covent Garden, it's as if I've traveled to my personal paradise. Shops line the quaint alley full of books—my favorite things after sex and pizza.

I could get lost and never want to be found. Except I *do* want to find Jude. What are the chances he'll be in one of these shops *right now?*

Maybe it's best to focus on my original mission. Even before I left the States, I wanted to go to the bookshop I'd visited as a kid. No, not that one with the medical textbooks.

Definitely not the children's bookstore with the stuffed dragon in the window.

And for sure it's not the shop with globes in the window.

When I've scoured nearly the whole alley, I'm convinced the store I camped out in a decade ago has closed.

Until a sign beckons me.

An Open Book.

It feels like déjà vu.

Peering inside, I breathe a sigh of relief. This is the store. Jude is probably history, and soon, he'll be a hazy memory of my first day in London—just some cute guy I met one afternoon.

A bell tinkles as I enter. I don't see a shopkeeper. Maybe they're in the back?

I browse the shelves, checking out row after row of colorful spines, stories in each one that lure me to read and also to write. I reach a row of works by Oscar Wilde, one of the greatest Irish writers ever. That dude was funny as fuck.

As I tip a copy of *The Importance of Being Earnest* into my hand, the thump of a hardback tome rattles a shelf behind me and I jerk my head.

Then I turn.

And wow.

This must be kismet.

Jude's paused in the act of sorting books, surprised to see me, it seems. And he looks—impossibly—even better than he did a few hours ago.

"You found the shop," he says, his lips twitching with the hint of a grin, his blue eyes full of mischief.

All at once, everything feels a little

heady and a lot possible. Like this is the start of something. My fingers tingle, and I'm not even sure why. But maybe it's just from this dizzying sense of . . . fate.

And fear.

I don't want to fuck this up. Life doesn't give you a lot of chances. So I don't answer him right away. "Well, I had a few clues," I finally say.

Maybe I was wrong. Maybe I *did* step off the plane and into my very own rom-com.

"It's good to be an amateur detective," he tosses back.

So that's how we're doing it—going toe to toe and quip to quip. Bring it on. "Who said anything about amateur?"

His lips curve into a sly grin. "Ohhh . . . you're a professional detective?"

"How else would I have found An Open Book?"

His eyes travel up and down my body. "Sheer determination."

I laugh. "Yes, a little bit of that, but

someone left a few hints. It was like a scavenger hunt. Maybe that's my new calling—scavenger hunting."

"Didn't know that was a thing. You do learn something new every day," he says. Then he makes that wildly sexy move again as he did outside TK Maxx —he coasts his teeth over that lower lip. I stifle a groan. My God, does he know what that does to a man?

Who am I kidding? Of course he does. A guy who looks, talks, stands like that—he's gorgeous and knows it.

Hell, he makes leaning against a shelf sexy.

"You know what I learned today?" I ask, plucking at my new Tetris shirt. It's nice and snug and makes my chest look good.

"Dying to know."

"That Angie's Vintage Duds does, in fact, have good clothes. Appreciate the tip."

"Would I lead you astray?"

That's an excellent question. I glance down at *The Importance of Being Earnest* in my hand as I hunt for retorts, then I look up, our gazes locking. "I have no idea, Jude. Would you?"

He laughs easily. Bet he does everything easily. Pose, walk, talk, read, live.

"Not when it comes to important matters like finding just the right shirt, and just the right store, and just the right book." He steps closer, taps the Wilde I'm holding. If an electrical charge could jump through pages, it just did. My skin is sizzling, almost like he touched me rather than paper.

"Like this book. Is that what you came to the store for?" Jude asks it so damn innocently, like he's goading me into admitting I came here for him.

Of course, I did. But two can play at this flirting game. I waggle the book. "I just needed to brush up on my Wilde."

"Naturally. You're just here for the books," he says, calling me on my patent lie.

"It's a bookstore. Why else would I come?" I counter.

"There couldn't be *any* other

reason," he says. "But I'd be a terrible shop assistant if I didn't help you find just the right Wilde." He takes his time with his speech so that each word can send a wicked charge through me.

They all do.

"Except, I don't even know your name," he adds.

I glance around. The shop is empty, except for a couple of young women parked on comfy chairs in the corner, flipping through guidebooks, maybe. They're wrapped up in their world. I hope they stay there for hours.

"I'm TJ," I say.

A laugh bursts from Jude.

"My name is funny to you?" I ask.

"That's so very American," he says.

"What do you know? I am American," I say. "And I know you don't do the whole initial thing here. Does that mean you prefer to be Jude the Third?"

Another laugh. "If I'd told you I was Jude the Third, I doubt you would've come looking for—" He sounds like he's about to say *me*, but he amends it, quickly shifting to, "All the Wildes. Besides, I'm just Jude."

But he's not just Jude.

He's not *just* at all.

I keep that thought locked up tight. "And if I'd told you what TJ stands for, you'd know exactly why some Americans prefer initials," I say.

His blue eyes sparkle with intrigue. "You have to tell me now, TJ." My name sounds like a bedroom whisper on his lips.

"You'll never get that out of me," I say, matching his breathless tone.

He arches a brow. "Never? Never ever, you say?"

I could dine on his charm. I could eat breakfast, lunch, and dinner on his wit. I never want to leave this store. We can play word badminton till after dark. I'll stop only when the lights go down, and we can do all the other things—the things I'm already picturing with that lush, red mouth of his.

"Never," I repeat, then take a long,

lingering moment. "Unless you have your ways."

He hums, a rumbly sound low in his throat. Then he taps his chin. "Perhaps I could guess. Thomas James?"

I shake my head. "Not even close."

"Theodore John." He makes a rolling gesture. "I could go all night."

"I hope so. And, perhaps, you should," I say.

Over drinks. Over sex. Over breakfast.

But the shop bell tinkles.

Jude groans as a customer strolls in. "I have to go wait on a customer."

And I have to make sure you and I go out tonight.

But before I can say *You'll find me here by the Oscar Wildes*, Jude adds, "Don't go anywhere, Thiago Jonas."

"You're not even warm," I say as he walks past me, brushing his shoulder against mine.

"But I bet you are," he whispers.

I try to stifle the hitch in my breath. But it's hard with this man, and his mouth, and his face, and my good fortune.

"Very," I say, low, just for him.

"Good," he says, then strides to the front of the store and chitchats with a customer. The whole time he ushers her around, my neck is warm, my head is hazy, and I feel like this is happening to some other guy. Like this is just a figment of my jet-lagged brain.

I flip open the book, turn it to one of my favorite scenes, and hear the lines in Jude's voice.

It's never sounded better.

A few minutes later, Jude returns, sliding up by my side to read over my shoulder, his breath near my ear. "*I hope you have not been leading a double life, pretending to be wicked and being good all the time. That would be hypocrisy.*" He stops before I melt, because yeah, that's the best I've ever heard this play. "Do you like Oscar Wilde?"

"Very much so," I say, trying to stay cool. "You?"

"A lot," he says, and neither one of us is talking about the Irish poet.

But I feel Wilde would approve of everything I'm about to do.

"Go out with me tonight, Jude," I say, as a tangle of heat rushes down my chest, curls into a knot in my belly.

"I was hoping you'd ask. *But . . .*" He pauses, and my stomach plummets. This is when he'll disappoint me. "I have to work till nine. Can you meet at nine-thirty?

That's it? That's the *but*? I would meet him at three in the morning. At noon. Now.

I keep all that eagerness to myself. "Yeah. Want to meet at a pub? Get a beer? That sounds so very English."

"And it also sounds so very good," he says. "Where are you staying?"

"Not far from here. My hotel's near Piccadilly Circus."

"Meet me at The Magpie."

"I'll be there."

He points to the book. "Is this the

edition you came for? The one with the two men in top hats?"

"It's perfect."

"Did you really want the book?"

I swallow roughly, meet his eyes, speak the whole truth. "I really want the book," I say, and it's not a lie. It also might have a double meaning.

As he heads to the counter, I follow him. I feel like I'd follow him anywhere, and that's a dangerous thought. But now's not the time for analyzing.

Now is a time for doing.

Jude rings me up, slides the card reader across the counter, then takes out his phone. After I swipe my credit card, he says, "And I believe you were going to give me your number, TJ."

As I slide him the card reader, he gives me his phone. I keep my head down, so he can't see the size of my smile as I tap in my digits then swivel the device back to him. Seconds later, he sends me a text.

Jude: Mark my words. I'll figure out what TJ stands for. I have my ways.

TJ: Just try them on me.

Then, since it's always good to leave them wanting more, I take the Wilde and go. As I walk off, I can see the rest of my days and nights in London in a whole new way.

Chapter Four

A Great Dick with A Great Dick

Jude

I've had dates that started worse.

There was the guy who turned out to be my second cousin, though thankfully learned of our interconnected family tree branches before we smacked lips. Then, there was another guy who informed me the second I sat down at the table that he liked to take cold baths before sex.

Give a bloke some food before you reveal your fetishes. I mean, that's just polite.

But let's not forget the man who cried the instant I arrived at the café. I don't even know why. He just blubbered for thirty minutes till I called him an Uber and sent him home.

With that precedent, a night out with a hot, but exhausted American likely won't crack the top-three worst dates. But when I catch sight of TJ through the window of The Magpie, yawning wide enough to fit a double-decker bus, I suspect the evening won't end the way I imagined—with *mutual finishing*.

Well, there are other uses for mouths.

I go into the packed bar and head straight for his booth, where he's reading the book he bought. "Usually, it takes a few beers before I bore my dates, so I'm ahead on that count," I say.

"Sorry about that," TJ says with a tired laugh as he sets the Wilde aside. "But I assure you, boredom is not the issue."

"It's past your bedtime?" I suspect that's why he's zonked.

A sheepish look flits across his tired eyes. "That obvious?"

"Yes, but you said it was your first day in London." I slide onto the dark wood bench across from him. On the wall above us hangs a vintage poster of London from a century ago.

"Who's the detective now?" TJ counters.

"It's a useful skill," I say drily, tapping my temple. "Remembering, that is."

"Sure is. And hey, if it helps, I haven't slept in more than twenty-four hours. But thanks for the heads-up that you're dull." TJ points to the door. "I'll just make my great escape right now."

"I don't think you're going to slip away just yet."

His eyebrows dart up. "And why is that, Just Jude?"

"Oh, I have a nickname already?"

"You made it easy."

I'd like to make a lot of things easy for him. Like, say, having me when he's not knackered. "And you've made it hard for me to figure out your real name."

"But you like it that way. *Hard*," he says.

I shrug coyly. "I do enjoy a hard man."

He chuckles, then he holds up a finger for a pause. "One sec." Grabbing his mobile, he quickly taps something out on the screen.

I peer over the table, intrigued. "Are you taking notes on our conversation?"

"It gave me an idea—what you just said." He finishes typing and sets his phone down, a little amused with his own notes.

That ratchets up my curiosity. "And, are you going to keep that idea all to yourself, like your real name? Or will you share?"

TJ gives a sly smile. "Depends on what I do with it," he answers in a tone that says *Let's leave it at that.*

Fair enough. I don't need to push him on his notetaking. People reveal things when they're ready. But I want him to reveal *something* to me. I have a hunch about it, but I'll have to get the answer out of him in a roundabout way. "Great table. Did you get here a while ago?"

"Yeah, I did," he says, scratching his jaw like he's playing at "laidback" too. "I mean, I didn't know how long it would take to walk here from my hotel, or whether the GPS directions are right, or whether The Magpie would be crowded since it's a Saturday night. So, I showed up a bit early."

The way he overexplains is endearing, and confirms my hunch that he was as eager to impress me with a good table as I was eager to find him earlier. Call me a glutton for compliments, but I do like knowing when someone's into me. I can blame my ex for that, I suppose.

"That's why I didn't think you'd slip away," I say. "Who'd want to give up such a great table?"

"Not me," he adds, as if he's trying not to smile.

A waitress swings by and asks us our poison. I pick a lager, while TJ opts for an ale. When she leaves, I'm tempted to confess I doubled back to Angie's to see him again. But if I admit I chased him to the thrift shop, he might put me in an Uber like I've blubbered to him.

I'd deserve it.

I play it cool instead, opting for a safer topic. "So, how are you finding London so far?"

He shrugs, all no big deal, but keeps those dark eyes on me. "It's not so bad. I guess we'll see if you can keep me up."

"That's a tall order. But I think I'm *up* to the task. I happen to be a scintillating conversationalist."

"Then, Just Jude, you really should

keep scintillating." Something about the way he says that—all faux naughty—rips a laugh straight from my chest. He cracks up too. "All right. Tell me for real about your first day in my hometown. Besides meeting a fabulous Englishman who has the same tastes."

"Thank God for that," TJ says, relieved.

"Same here. It's always a welcome moment when you know you're not barking up the wrong tree," I say.

"I prefer the right trees. And England is . . . pretty good so far. Even though the airline lost my bags, my room wasn't ready, and I had nothing clean to wear until this afternoon. Also, apparently, I can't stop yawning." Another one racks him as the blonde server returns with our drinks.

"Here's your lager and your ale," she says, setting down the glasses. "Shall I start a tab for you?"

"Yes," TJ says, just as I say, "No."

She holds up her hands to show

she's not getting involved. "I'll let you gentlemen sort that out."

I hand her my credit card. "Here you go, love. We're all set."

"Thank you," she says, then spins on her heel.

I turn back to TJ, who's crossing his arms. Oh, no, no, no. He's not getting it. "You think when you said yes, and I said no, that I meant I was taking off straight away?"

He scoffs in denial. "It's all good. I'm happy to call it a night," he says, so damn nonchalant.

"I'm not letting you get away that quickly."

Like that, his cool demeanor cracks. A smile breaks through.

I get up, move to his side of the booth, and slide in next to him. When we're thigh to thigh, his breath hitches, then it catches as I drape an arm around him.

"Are you trapping me?" he asks.

"Yes. Is it working?"

"Depends on what you want to do."

"Keep you here for this drink."

He's quiet for a few seconds. "It's working quite well."

"Good. I'd hate to be presumptuous if it wasn't working."

He clears his throat. "You should be very presumptuous."

"Then I'll presume about other things too." I curl my hand over that big, strong shoulder that feels so fucking good. I do like a man who's bigger than I am, broader than I am. Who can climb over me and pin me down.

"What sort of things?" he asks, a little breathy.

Ah, fuck it. He's probably only in town for a short while. Might as well enjoy this while it lasts. "Things like . . . tomorrow."

That wins me the start of a smile, then the slight turn of his face toward me. "What are you presuming about tomorrow?"

"That I'll see you again," I tell him. "When you're not falling asleep. When you're not yawning into your fucking beer."

With a laugh, he rolls his eyes then leans back in the booth. "I'm only a *little* tired," he says, so much gravel in his voice now.

"That's why I gave her my card. That's why I said we were set. So we can have this one drink to your first night in town. And something more tomorrow."

He nods a few times, clearly liking my plan. If he only knew all the dirty plans I have for him tomorrow. "I'll drink to something more," he says, and we lift glasses and clink.

"Cheers," I say, then drink and lick my lips. "So, what brings you to London? Give me the two-minute version since I'm going to put you in an Uber soon."

"I'm writing an exposé on book-shops," he says, deadpan.

"So, this is all a ruse to get me to reveal the hidden secrets of the shelves?"

"Seems to be working too. I already uncovered critical details, like how much you adore helping customers and which edition of *The Importance of Being Earnest* is your favorite."

I try to remember when I told him but draw a blank. "I didn't tell you the one you bought was my favorite."

"You didn't have to tell me. I figured it out from your clues," he says, and this man would make a good detective because he's spot on.

"Perhaps all this Sherlock Holmes work of yours brought you to London then?"

He takes another drink and casually sets down the glass. "Or maybe I'm a Wilde scholar here in London to research the man."

"But we're all Wilde scholars, aren't we?"

"Excellent point," he says, then his tone shifts like he's letting down his guard. "When I was in high school and first learned he was gay, I checked out all Oscar Wilde's works from the library. Devoured them. I've read this one several times." He taps the top hat cover. "Maybe I felt I should have an affinity. Do you know what I mean?"

"I do—on both counts. And probably that's why I was the most excited I've ever been when I was cast as Jack Worthing in uni." I pause to replay in my head what I just said. "I hope I didn't sound like a braggart then. I was truly thrilled."

"Not at all. I can completely understand that excitement." This is our first stripped-down moment, free of flirting or trying to impress the other. It's nice, and I like it, but I don't want it to last too long. I don't want too much closeness in my life, and I doubt TJ does either, judging by how quickly he returns to the banter.

"And is that your way of telling me you have a second career?" he asks. "That you're an actor?"

"Yes. Clever, isn't it? How I dropped that in?"

"Very much so. So, the bookstore thing, then?"

"I moonlight there. Bills and all," I say, offhand. I don't want to reveal the full extent of my acting dreams. Don't want to let on that I spend my days auditioning for hoover adverts and bit parts on web shows and every single fringe theater production that might be right for me. That I'm chasing a wildly unlikely dream of making it big in film and on stage. He'd probably laugh. "And I'm guessing you're a writer?"

A surprised laugh bursts from the man next to me. "It's as obvious as me being tired?"

"Pretty obvious, TJ." I don't go into how I caught on. It'd be evident I'm paying too much attention to every detail of him—like how he sometimes takes his time with his words like he's writing them out in his head first. Rather than say that, I tease, "Your whole look kind of screams writer."

Okay, I can't help it.

His jaw drops, and he gestures to

himself. "Am I disheveled, unshowered, and dressed in sweats? No. Not to cast aspersions on other writers, mind you."

I lean closer and whisper, "I won't tell all the other writers in the world that you mock their wardrobes."

"Thank you so very much. Anyway, you're right. I am a writer—well, I'm a business reporter—and my news organization sent me here to cover the financial markets."

"Ah, stocks, bonds, money, money, money," I say.

"That's the gist of my days," TJ says, then takes a breath like he's not quite sure if he wants to say the next thing. But then he goes for it. "I'll be here for a year."

I flinch in surprise. "That's a long time."

He laughs, but it's defensive. "You're rethinking that offer for tomorrow, aren't you?"

Am I? Does the score change with him living here rather than being on holiday?

I'm not in the market for a relationship after the way my last one ended. But first dates aren't the best time to lay down the rules of my solo road.

I keep my answer on the level—the physical level. "I'm thinking I'm still quite interested in seeing what's underneath this writer's garb."

He laughs. "So, I do dress like a writer."

"A little bit. But that isn't stopping me from wanting to touch what's under the Tetris T-shirt," I say playfully, plucking at the fabric near his belly.

I'm so very tempted to check out his abs. But I don't want to be handsy. I'll just have to imagine what they're like. Or maybe not, because TJ grabs my hand and places it on his stomach.

Oh, yes. They're as firm as I imagined.

TJ gives a slight smirk. "Figured this was easier than you surreptitiously trying to check out my abs."

"Was playing with your shirt what we'd call surreptitious?"

"Not in the motherfucking least," he says.

This is my chance to turn the tables on him, to grab his palm, and set it on my stomach.

But he lifts his hand and takes another drink.

Maybe he wants to leave me wanting him more. And I do want TJ, even this tired version—make that dog-tired because there he goes again with another yawn.

"All right, stud. It's well past your bedtime," I tell him.

"It's not even five in New York," he protests.

"And yet, you look like you could sleep for days," I say.

"I do like sleep, but I also like doing other things in bed," he says, his voice husky and hopeful.

"Tomorrow, Troy Jett," I say and ruffle his hair. I like touching him. *A lot.*

"Troy Jett? Please."

"It was worth a shot."

He arches a dubious brow.

"Promise me something. Promise me you'll never date a douche named Troy Jett."

"That is a particularly dickish name," I say.

He hums, tapping his chin. "Why is dick an insult?"

"That's an excellent question, considering how much I love it," I say, giving a little roll of the tongue with those last few words.

"That's why it should be a compliment of the highest order," TJ adds. "Instead of saying *he's a dick* when someone is a jerk, we should save *he's a dick* for a really awesome dude."

"Like, if I met a rather handsome stud, I'd say *I met a great dick today*." I take a beat to adopt a thoughtful expression. "At least, I think he's a great dick," I say, feigning worry. "What if he's not?"

TJ sighs heavily. "That'd be such a shame if the guy you think is a dick turns out to be a not-dick. But I'll let you in on a secret. I have a feeling this dude you met is definitely a dick. Like a big, huge dick. The biggest dick."

I groan, half in the promise of pleasure, half in amusement. "But I won't say I hope he has a big dick. Because, sure, size is nice and all. But great dicks come in all sizes. It's not the length or the girth, but what a great dick can do with a great dick."

TJ laughs, long and a little slaphappy. "You have a way with words too. And I will drink to your ode to all shapes and sizes," he says, and we toast once more.

Soon, we take our last sips of beer, reaching the end of the date. But before I can say good night, TJ leans into me and brushes a kiss onto my cheek.

I freeze and moan at the same time.

I didn't expect a kiss, and I definitely don't want it to end. His lips are utterly delicious on my skin. I close my eyes and revel in the barely-there stroke of his soft lips down to my jaw, where he's more insistent, a little rougher, that stubble scraping my chin in the best way.

I shudder out a breath. He lays a hand on my other cheek, holds me in place. "If you're a good dick, I'll give you a good night kiss," he whispers, and I'm so damn glad I lost the Cleaneroo gig. If the casting director had asked for a callback on the spot, I'd have missed my chance to run into TJ outside a discount shop.

"I'll be the best," I say, and I'm tempted to turn into his lips. To get lost in one of those endless, dreamy kisses I suspect he can give.

But I'm acutely aware of the power of waiting.

I've never edged with kisses. I plan to tonight.

A few minutes later, we're outside The Magpie. With the book in hand, he gestures in the direction of his hotel. "See you tomorrow sometime," he says.

"Text me when you're up, Sleeping Beauty," I say, nibbling the edge of my mouth absently for a second.

TJ stares wantonly at me, then steps closer. He's mere inches away. "You do this thing where you bite your lip, and it kind of drives me crazy." He drags his thumb along the corner of my mouth then chases it with his lips, giving me one more kiss right there. A spark sprints through me from that barest touch.

TJ steps away, walks backward, lifts his free hand to wave. "Goodnight, Just Jude."

"Welcome to London, Tobias Jangle."

With a smile, TJ turns and strolls into the London evening. The whole way home, I think of great dicks. Because that was the best goodnight kiss I've ever had, and it was also the most innocent.

ALSO BY LAUREN BLAKELY

FULL PACKAGE, the #1 New York Times Bestselling romantic comedy!

BIG ROCK, the hit New York Times Bestselling standalone romantic comedy!

THE SEXY ONE, a New York Times Bestselling standalone romance!

THE KNOCKED UP PLAN, a multi-week USA Today and Amazon Charts Bestselling standalone romance!

MOST VALUABLE PLAYBOY, a sexy multi-week USA Today Bestselling sports romance! And its companion sports romance, MOST LIKELY TO SCORE!

WANDERLUST, a USA Today Bestselling contemporary romance!

COME AS YOU ARE, a Wall Street Journal and multi-week USA Today Bestselling contemporary romance!

PART-TIME LOVER, a multi-week USA Today Bestselling contemporary romance!

UNBREAK MY HEART, an emotional second chance USA Today Bestselling contemporary romance!

BEST LAID PLANS, a sexy friends-to-lovers USA Today Bestselling romance!

The Heartbreakers! The USA Today and WSJ Bestselling rock star series of standalone!

P.S. IT'S ALWAYS BEEN YOU, a sweeping, second chance romance!

MY ONE WEEK HUSBAND, a sexy standalone romance!

CONTACT

You can find Lauren on Twitter at LaurenBlakely3, Instagram at LaurenBlakelyBooks, Facebook at LaurenBlakelyBooks, or online at LaurenBlakely.com. You can also email her at laurenblakelybooks@gmail.com

Made in United States
North Haven, CT
07 February 2023

32126754R00071